MIRIAM AND THE SASQUATCH

For Linda Whitmore —

who lives out in Sasquatch country.

— EAK

Thanks for all the support.

You have helped me to be as strong as a Sasquatch.

— TA

Apples & Honey Press

An Imprint of Behrman House Publishers

Millburn, New Jersey 07041

www.applesandhoneypress.com

ISBN 978-1-68115-581-4

Text copyright © 2022 by Eric A. Kimmel

Illustrations copyright © 2022 by Behrman House

Library of Congress Control Number: 2021949543

Design by Elynn Cohen

Edited by Dena Neusner

Printed in China

1 3 5 7 9 8 6 4 2

0822/B1895/A6

MIRIAM AND THE SASQUATCH

by Eric A. Kimmel   Illustrated by Tamara Anegon

MIRIAM looked over the apple orchard. Autumn leaves were turning yellow and gold. The beehives were full of honey. The apples were ready to pick. Rosh Hashanah was coming.

Miriam imagined all the apples and honey on her family's holiday table, as she waited for their guests to arrive.

Miriam didn't come to the orchard just to pick apples.

She also came to practice blowing her shofar. She could practice in the orchard without hurting anyone's ears.

Miriam stood under an apple tree. She took a breath and blew.

She heard a sound above her head. It wasn't a shofar.

Munch! Crunch! Munch! Crunch!

What was making that noise? Miriam looked up into the apple tree.

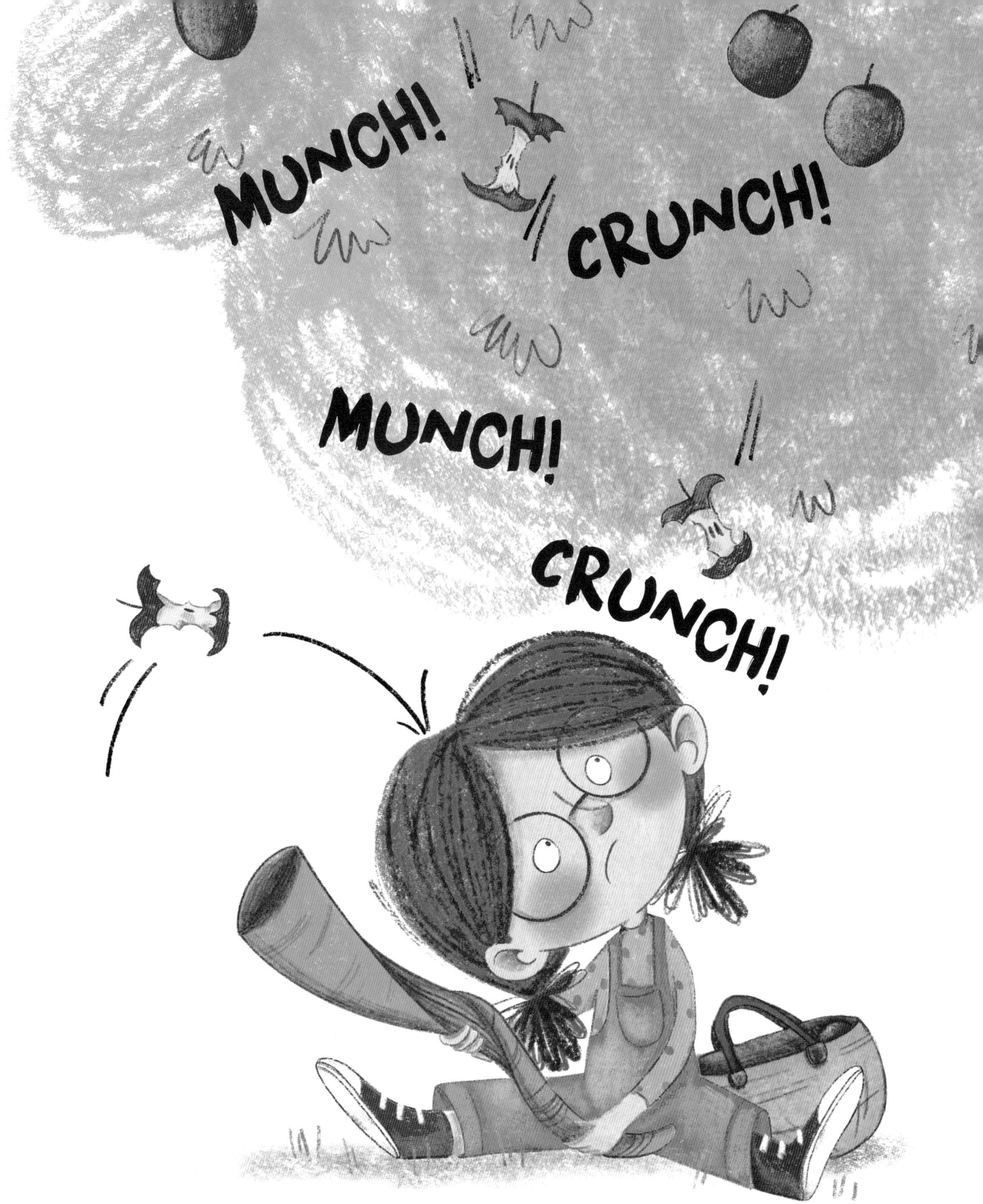
MUNCH!
CRUNCH!
MUNCH!
CRUNCH!

There sat a Sasquatch, munching away at the apples.

"Stop eating our apples! We need them for Rosh Hashanah!" Miriam shouted.

The Sasquatch stared at her. It went back to eating apples.

"Leave our apples alone!"
Miriam shook her fist
at the Sasquatch.

The Sasquatch shook its fist at
Miriam. It kept eating apples.

"That Sasquatch will eat all our apples," Miriam said. "How can I get it to go away?"

Miriam remembered a story from the Bible. "If a shofar can bring down the walls of Jericho, I bet it can chase away a Sasquatch!"

Miriam raised the shofar.
She blew as loud as she could.

The Sasquatch stared at Miriam.
It cupped its hands to its mouth
and gave out a mighty howl.

Miriam had to cover her ears. The Sasquatch went back to eating apples.

"That's enough! You can't eat all our apples!" Miriam picked up an apple. She threw it at the Sasquatch.

The Sasquatch caught the apple.

It threw it back at Miriam.

Miriam ducked. The apple whizzed over her head.

It slammed into a beehive.

Bees swarmed out of the hive. The Sasquatch jumped out of the tree and ran for the pond. Miriam ran, too. She'd be safe in the pond. Bees don't swim.

Miriam slipped on an apple. Down she went. Angry bees swarmed around her.

"Help!" Miriam shouted.

The Sasquatch turned around. It picked up Miriam and raced for the pond.

The Sasquatch jumped in the pond. It stayed in
the pond with Miriam until the bees went away.

"You saved me from the bees even after I threw apples at you. Even when I wouldn't let you eat any. I didn't even think that you might be hungry," Miriam said to the Sasquatch.

The Sasquatch shrugged. It held out its hand to Miriam. Hand in hand, they walked back to the orchard. The Sasquatch climbed an apple tree. This time it didn't go "Munch! Crunch! Munch! Crunch!"

It picked apples and handed them to Miriam.

"We can pick apples together," said Miriam. "And you can eat as many as you want."

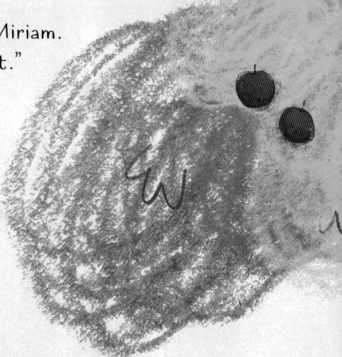

Rosh Hashanah arrived. Miriam helped her family get ready for the holiday. There was challah and rugelach and honey cake.

And apples and honey for everyone—family and friends, old . . .

and new.

NOTE TO READERS

The germ of this story came to me while on a birding trip in Borneo. I heard a story about a farmer whose durian fruit plantation was being raided by an orangutan who wouldn't go away.

That started me thinking. What if I moved the story to my own part of the world, Northwest Oregon? We have apple orchards—but no orangutans. What we have had over the years are several reported sightings of Sasquatch, otherwise known as Bigfoot.

A Sasquatch is a large hairy primate that is said to live in forested areas and walk on two legs. Like the Chupacabra, the Yeti, and the Loch Ness Monster, there is no scientific proof that such a creature exists.

It does, however, make for a good story—especially at Rosh Hashanah time when we traditionally eat apples and honey. The sweetness of honey combines with the tart taste of apples, and together they remind us of the warmth and sweetness of the past year, as well as the times that were not so good or when we failed to act as we should. They remind us not to forget those who have no warm home or holiday table; for they are also part of our family—all over the world, whether human or Sasquatch.